Hello, Jimmy!

Anna Walker

CLARION BOOKS I Houghton Mifflin Harcourt I Boston New York

Clarion Books ▪ 3 Park Avenue, New York, New York 10016 ▪ Copyright © 2021 by Anna Walker ▪ All rights reserved. ▪ For information about permission to reproduce selections from this book, write to trade.permissions@hmhco.com or to Permissions, Houghton Mifflin Harcourt Publishing Company, 3 Park Avenue, 19th Floor, New York, New York 10016. ▪ Clarion Books is an imprint of Houghton Mifflin Harcourt Publishing Company. ▪ hmhbooks.com The illustrations in this book were created using gouache and pencil on watercolor paper. ▪ The text was set in Galaxie Polaris. ▪ Library of Congress Cataloging-in-Publication Data: Names: Walker, Anna, author, illustrator. ▪ Title: Hello, Jimmy! / by Anna Walker. ▪ Description: New York : Clarion Books, [2021] | Audience: Ages 4 to 7. | Audience: Grades K–1. | Summary: "A funny, noisy parrot comes into Jack's world and brings him closer to his dad in an unexpected and moving way" —Provided by publisher. ▪ Identifiers: LCCN 2019036637 (print) | LCCN 2019036638 (ebook) | ISBN 9780358193586 (hardcover) | ISBN 9780358360902 (ebook) ▪ Subjects: CYAC: Fathers and sons—Fiction. | Parrots—Fiction. | Loneliness—Fiction. ▪ Classification: LCC PZ7.W15214 Hel 2021 (print) | LCC PZ7.W15214 (ebook) | DDC [E]—dc23 ▪ LC record available at https://lccn.loc.gov/2019036637 LC ebook record available at https://lccn.loc.gov/2019036638 ▪ Manufactured in China ▪ SCP 10 9 8 7 6 5 4 3 2 1 4500811158

This book is dedicated to my brother.
And for the child who feels lost,
may you feel found
and know you are loved.

When Jack stayed at his dad's house,
they made tacos.
And milkshakes, too.

Sometimes they talked.

And sometimes they didn't.

Jack's dad liked to tell funny jokes,
but he hadn't told one in a while.

Jack couldn't be there
all the time.
The house was so quiet.
He wondered if his dad
was lonely.

Jack knew what that felt like.

One Tuesday night when Jack arrived,
his dad had a surprise.

Jack didn't like surprises.

"His name is Jimmy.
I found him on the doorstep
after the storm last week," said Dad.

Hello, Jimmy!

Bye-bye, Jimmy!

Be good, Jimmy!

"Don't call me Jimmy!
My name's Jack.
Your name's Jimmy."

Dad loved Jimmy.

Dad told his jokes
and Jimmy laughed.

"He can walk, he can talk,
and he can even do the dishes," said Dad.
"He's amazing!"

Jack wished he was amazing too.

Jimmy was loud.

Squaawwk!

He was funny,

clever . . .

Hello, Jimmy!

Love you!

and full of surprises.
Everyone loved Jimmy.

Now Dad had a friend
to keep him company,
and the house was not
quiet anymore.

Ssshhhh!

When Jack turned out the light
and closed his eyes,
all he could hear was
the rustle of Jimmy's feathers.

Then morning arrived.

Jack had to find Jimmy.

"Jimmy?

Hello, Jimmy?"

Jack called and called.

But the only voice he heard was his own.

"Jimmy's not here, Dad.

He's gone."

"I am not looking for Jimmy."

"I am looking for Jack."

When Jack stayed at his dad's house,
sometimes they talked.

And sometimes they didn't.

Jack hoped he might see Jimmy again one day . . .

. . . even if it was a surprise.